# When the Doves Coo

*A Prequel to The Two Valleys Series*

Mary Armstrong

Enchanted Writing Company

ISBN:978-1-7371545-3-2

Cover design by White Rabbit Arts at The Historical Fiction Company

Library of Congress Control Number: case #1-11002979751

Printed in the United States of America

# Author's Note

"When the Doves Coo" was written between books one and two of "The Two Valleys" series. It's a wonderful story on its own merits — about the life of a family member that doesn't fit with his parents and brothers and sister. In essence, it could take place anywhere and at any time.

In this case, it gives the reader some depth to the reasons that Jesús — known by the common nickname of "Chuy" to his family — was sent to live with the Fountains in New Mexico Territory in 1886.

If this is your first acquaintance with Jesús, I hope you will continue to follow his coming-of-age story set against the ten years of history that led to the notorious and unsolved murders of Colonel Albert J. Fountain and his eight-year-old son in 1896.

"Chuy, you must not resist the tequila. It will stop you from feeling much of the pain when I fix your bone." I nodded, realizing that the burning sensation would be better than the pain I felt earlier. He tipped the bottle to my mouth again, saying, "Breath through your nose now, Chuy … that's right … slow, even breaths." Soon I was feeling drowsy, and the *Padre* took the bottle from my lips. That was all I remembered.

I awakened to a pounding headache and instinctively tried to pull my left hand to my head, but I couldn't move it. At first, I thought the *Padre* had decided to cut off my arm. It was dark. My mother appeared from the darkness and shushed me as she put her hand across my arm. "No *mijo*," she whispered. "You mustn't move your arm. The *Padre* said to keep you in bed and for you to keep your arm still for a week. He will come back tomorrow and check on you. Here" — she tilted my head up and gave me a sip of a syrupy liquid from a small bottle — "the *Padre* said this will help your headache and make you relax."

"What is it, *Madre*?" I breathed.

"The *Padre* said it is marijuana … now lay back and relax. You will feel better tomorrow."

I did feel better the next day and when the *Padre* came to see me, he brought a slate and chalk. He held the slate while I wrote — well, tried to write — the alphabet with my right hand. At first, the letters were barely readable, but as the week progressed my writing improved, and by the time I was able to get up from bed, my writing was much better. During his visits, Padre Rosales asked me to read to him. We talked about the books I had read, of which I only had a few. By the time the week was out he had convinced me to come back for more lessons. He told me he would teach me English and arithmetic.

When I was able to leave my bed, my mother said, "You can feed the chickens in the mornings and herd the goats into the barn after supper. As your arm heals you can weed and water the kitchen garden and eventually carry firewood and water for the kitchen." Even doing all that I still had time for my studies and some free time. This helped me feel as though I was contributing something.

Jacinto and Miguel were very close. When they would come in from the fields — as they did Monday through Saturday evenings for supper — Jacinto acted like he was ten years older than his eighteen years and Miguel followed him around like his little puppy. Often they would jostle and tease each other as they approached the adobe. If they noticed me it was to mock me with '*mija*' this and '*mija*' that. I suppose I deserved it since I took my lessons and helped my mother with chores around the adobe while they did the hard work of planting, watering, weeding, and harvesting our crops.

My father would smile, pat me on the head after they passed and say, "Don't pay any attention to them, *mijo*, they are only letting off steam after a long hard day's work." On Saturday evenings, Jacinto and Miguel would join our father on the *porche* for tequila or a special wine after supper. I would stay inside at our table with my books, reading by candlelight until my mother called for me to go to bed.

Angelina, my little sister, seemed always 'underfoot' of my mother. She clung to her apron strings even as she hurried to the *letrinas*. Sometimes Angelina would ask me to play make-believe. I did for a while, but mother didn't like it and so I stopped. Most of the time I would go outside and find Facile. He would be grazing somewhere, but when I called "FACILE!" and whistled the way mother had taught me, he would come trotting and hee-hawing his greeting. Our farmyard dog, who we simply called 'Pero', would come running from another direction and the three of us would venture off into the tank father and my brothers had dug to water the stock, or if there was plenty of time we might go to the bosque next to the Rio Bravo where the river and trees and made it cooler.

## When the Doves Coo

Sometimes I would bring my lessons to the bosque, but on the hottest days, when the river was little more than a creek I would strip, and Facile, Pero and I would go swimming. At first, I didn't think Facile would swim, but soon he and Pero would jump and splash and we would swim across the deeper channel to the United States. After swimming back, I would lay out in the sun and dry before dressing and going into the shade where I would read Don Quixote aloud in English to Facile and Pero. Sometimes when I stumbled over words or practiced my pronunciation repeatedly, Facile would twitch his ears and hee-haw while Pero would put his front paws over his ears. There was one passage in Don Quixote that seemed to especially strike a chord with Pero. Perhaps it was because I would recite it in a singsong tone, or because it had a repetitive sound. The passage was:

"There is a time for some things, and a time for all things; a time for great things, and a time for small things."

For some reason, it made Pero howl — perhaps it was because if there was "a time for all things" then it wasn't necessary to write "a time for some things", or any other of the things he wrote about.

Facile wasn't very big, but he was strong and he loved to play with me and Pero. Sometimes we would play a game that involved tracking. I would tie them to a tree in the bosque and rub some of a treat that I had brought for them on the bottom of my sandals. After hiding their treats, a distance away, I would take off my sandals and return to release Facile and Pero. Between the two of them, they would find the treats in no time and then come running back to me for more.

Last winter, someone shot Pero and he died. Facile and I found him on the mesa. My father said he was probably disturbing someone's chickens or harassing their sheep or goats. For a time, I worried that I might have somehow done something that led him to do such a thing.

Facile and I stopped doing the treat hide-and-seek game. It wasn't the same without Pero, and Facile wasn't nearly as good at following a trail. Instead, I would bring my serape or a small blanket and put it over Facile's eyes. I would run around and around him and then stop somewhere nearby. At first, Facile lifted his head and tried to shake off the makeshift blindfold, but I would coax him to me, take it off and reward him with a treat. Eventually, it got to be a game between us and he didn't resist the serape. The closer he would get to me, the more his floppy ears twitched and when I removed the serape he would put his head over my shoulder and lean against my head with a hug.

Nearly all my fun had something to do with our animals. The most fun of the year came when the young goats could stand and run early each spring. They had a crazy way of running, hopping, bumping into each other and knocking each other over, getting up and jumping onto a pile of hay or stack of wood, and jumping down onto one of the other kids which would result in a separate group of running and jumping goats. I often found myself bending over in laughter with no one to share in the fun.

### *March 1886*

A few years passed and I settled into a daily routine of chores, study, and a little fun with Facile or watching the goats. We followed the Catholic Church's edict of Sunday being for rest, but we did not regularly worship at the little chapel where Padre Rosales preached.

When I returned to my lessons and we had established a relationship, *Padre* scolded me for not coming to church every Sunday. "Do you think that attending only the Solemnity celebrations is sufficient devotion to get you into heaven? You and your family will most certainly go to hell if you do not attend regularly!"

Mother had told me to expect the *Padre* to say something to me but I was stunned. His remarks seemed to come out of thin air and now, so many years later, I realize that he was troubled by the fact that he was tutoring someone that he considered unworthy.

## When the Doves Coo

All week I thought about what to do. I knew that I couldn't talk to my father about it. He would just get angry. Mother was caught in between just as I was. Father had made it clear that we would only attend church on a few special days. Finally, I decided that I would go by myself.

The following Sunday, while my family was outside enjoying the morning air, I dressed in my best clothes and walked to the chapel. I arrived late and I couldn't find a place to sit. As I stood in the aisle at the back of the church scanning the finely crafted pews, Padre Rosales caught my eye and motioned me to a spot in the front row where people I didn't know made room for me. As I walked up the aisle, I felt like the eyes of the entire congregation were upon me but I was so scared I couldn't look around. Padre kept glancing at me during the mass and smiling, which just made things worse. I knew that everyone was wondering who was this boy the Padre knew that wandered into the church alone? Those that knew my parents must have thought much less of them for sending their son alone. It was a mistake and as soon as Padre Rosales crossed himself for the final time I stood and walked quickly to the back of the chapel before running away. I ran as hard as I could and got so tired that I stumbled, fell, and ripped a hole in the knee of my good pants. By the time I got home my freshly laundered clothes were dirty, torn, and damp with my sweat.

"*Madre con Dios*! Chuy! What have you done?" cried my mother.

Behind her, in the Italian my father sometimes reverted to when he was excited, yelled, "*Mio Dio! Tu goffo idiota*!"

I was out of breath and huffed and puffed my way through: "I went to … church and … they all stared … at me and … *Padre* kept looking … "

"Never mind, *mijo*," interjected father. "I'm sorry I called you a clumsy oaf. I understand what happened at the church. Tomorrow you stay home from your studies, and I will have a talk with that *Padre*."

I didn't know what he might say to Padre Rosales, but I did remember him previously telling mother, "Latin is a dead language and if we could not understand what the *Padre* was asking God to do for us, why would we need to be there? They use it to impose power over us — to make us think they are closer to God than we are, but they aren't."

The next day father wore his work clothes to visit the rectory. When mother asked him why he wasn't changing to his best, he smirked, "Why should a man that works hard six days a week pay tribute to a man that hardly lifts a finger to support himself?"

When he returned, he said nothing and simply went back to the fields. That evening, while he sat sipping wine on the *porche* in the cool air I went out and asked him what *Padre* had said.

"My son, you mustn't worry about what the *Padre* said nor about what I told him. All you need to know is that this is behind you … and the *Padre* will not bother you about attending church anymore. You will resume your lessons tomorrow. However, if his demeanor changes or he isn't as devoted to his tutoring as he was before, you are to come to me immediately. Is that understood?"

"Yes sir, but …"

"No, Chuy, it doesn't concern you and it was wrong of the *Padre* to put this on your shoulders. We will still attend church when we choose and he will not say anything to you about it anymore."

*July 1886*

My session with Padre Rosales had been very strange. On the way home, I couldn't get his drilling me about my name out of my mind. I'm not planning to travel. And why did he say it was about preparing me for life?

## When the Doves Coo

Summers on the farm were difficult and other than a daily siesta, the work went on from dawn to dusk. My father and brothers were in the fields and my mother made and mended clothes, taught reading and writing to Angelina, tended to cleaning, slaughtering, and cooking. Any leftover time went to embroidering which she occasionally sold.

A week or so after the *Padre* drilled me about what name to use in different situations, I arrived home from my lessons at siesta time. I came around the corner of our adobe to see mother and father huddled over the small table on the *porche* talking quietly. It surprised me because father always napped after the midday meal until it was time to go back to the fields. When he and mother saw me, they immediately stood up and asked how my lessons were. In all the years I had been going to see Padre Rosales, my father had only asked this once and that was when, at supper, I mentioned we were studying farming terms in English. Mother asked occasionally, but from the day of my discussion about my name with the *Padre*, her interest heightened.

Just before supper, I looked over at my little sister and realized she wasn't so little anymore. She was my height and weighed more than me. That meant I was the smallest person in my family. I decided I needed to eat more, so I ate everything I could and took seconds like my brothers, but after a few weeks, it didn't seem to matter and so I went back to eating as I had previously.

I began to worry that I might be a midget, but when I asked the *Padre*, he said, "No my son, you are not a midget. You have none of the characteristics of those blessed little people. You are just small for your age — you will grow."

About the time I had the discussion with the *Padre*, a letter arrived from mother's sister in the United States. The name we called her, Mia Tia, was an example of the mixed-up 'Spalian' that happened in our home. Mia Tia didn't write often, but when she did, her letter would be passed around to all of us. This time there was no passing of the letter, and no one asked why. Strange.

Finally, after a few days of stewing over not seeing the letter, I asked, "*Madre*, why are you not passing the letter for us to read?"

"Oh *mijo*, it isn't anything that you children should concern yourselves about … it … is for us adults." That satisfied me, but then a month later another letter arrived from Mia Tia and again it wasn't passed around. Two consecutive letters that were only for the adults? Something was happening — but what?

Angelina started tagging along with me when I did my chores. It was nice to have someone to talk to and she asked lots of questions. We laughed together at the goat kids that were growing up, but still playful — and that was nice. One day when we were watching the kids tumble and chase, I asked Angelina if she knew what the letters from Mia Tia were about. She shrugged.

"Well, something is wrong don't you think? We always get to read the letters from Mia Tia."

Angelina shook her head. "All I know is that I'm going to have my own room soon. I've been complaining about sleeping in the main room and *Madre* said I would have a room to myself soon. She told me I would have to do chores though, but I'm happy to help."

I didn't know what to think. Maybe Papa was going to add on a room? Or maybe it was something that had to do with me. Was Angelina taking over my chores? Is that why she was tagging along with me every day?

A week later, I was in the bosque with Facile and I saw Jacinto go toward the Rio Bravo to cool off. I knew he had been courting the Rodriguez girl pretty hard. Maybe he would marry soon and he would leave the house and that was how Angelina would get her own room.

As he waded into the river, I caught his attention. "Jacinto!" He turned to me and waved as though dismissing me. "Wait … wait …" It appeared he would just ignore me and my final word "please" came out as almost a whisper. He dove into the slow-moving river and dunked his head again and again while I sat down on the bank and threw rocks into the water downstream. Facile stood next to me, nuzzling my shoulder. I felt like crying.

When I got up to walk back to the shade, Jacinto yelled to me, but I ignored him and walked into the shady bosque. Jacinto followed without me knowing.

"What is it, *mija*?"

He startled me and replied angrily, "Why do you call me that? Don't you know it hurts already that I am too small to do my part? I want to, you know … more than anything!"

"I'm sorry mi … Chuy. I'm only teasing. You know, Miguel and I like to tease each other … we even call each other names!"

I was beyond wanting to talk and I just waved him away from me and I bowed my head in shame.

He started to leave but stopped. "No! Now tell me what is bothering you … WHAT!"

I tilted my head just enough to see him through the hair hanging over my forehead. "Are you marrying the Rodriguez girl?"

"What?" He shook his head in confusion. "Not anytime soon, I think. But, why does it matter to you?"

I looked up at him. "Angelina says she is getting her own room before long and I thought …"

"You thought that if I was moving out then there would be a room for her. I see, but no, no, I have not asked Belén yet."

I thought for a moment, as Jacinto leaned over and ran his fingers through his hair trying to remove as much of the Rio Bravo as he could. "Well, do you know if Papa is going to add on another room?"

"If he is, he hasn't told me about it, but you worry too much. What are you thinking, that they are going to throw you out?" And then he laughed, and it hurt, and I looked away as tears gathered in the bottom of my eyes. He stopped laughing but just looked at me and I got up and called Facile as I walked back toward the river.

After I walked a dozen steps or so, I turned back and yelled, "Well, I hope they are sending me away so I can find people that love me!" It scared Facile and he trotted back toward home. I hid in the brambles, ashamed and not wanting to face Jacinto. He came to look for me, but I was too ashamed to face him and he didn't see me and said nothing.

After that, I didn't want to talk to any of them and when Angelina came with me as I did chores, I said, "Why are you always following me around? Leave me alone!"

It was the middle of the summer, and my father and brothers spent the mornings and evenings in the fields watering and weeding. They took siestas in the cool adobe after working into the midday heat. Facile and I no longer visited the water tank my father and brothers dug, for it had dried up with cracks in the silty soil so large I could fit my fist in them. But the bosque and Rio Bravo remained cool and wet, although much lower than in the spring when runoff from the mountains far to the north often created floods. I never went home at midday as my father and brothers did. I read to Facile and completed *Padre*'s assignments and napped during the heat of the day.

I had made a fishing pole from a willow branch, some cord, and a hook I had fashioned. Sometimes, if I was hungry, I would fish. If I caught something, I would build a small fire and cook it, but mostly I didn't get hungry, or if I did, I wouldn't eat because I thought I was punishing my family by becoming even skinnier and weaker.

Whatever I did, didn't seem to matter. Life went on for my family as it had for years. I rarely said anything unless someone spoke to me and I left the adobe in the mornings as soon as I could. Sometimes mother would ask if something was bothering me, but I would just smile and say, "Of course not, *Madre*. I was just thinking about my lessons." If she asked why we were never home, I would say, "Facile and I just like to be in the bosque while I am studying."

After a while, I didn't think she accepted those explanations, but I guess she didn't know what else to say and so nothing more was said. As you might imagine, a certain uneasiness settled over my entire existence. I became numb to my surroundings and ignored everyone. I withdrew into a world that included Facile and a barely tolerated Padre Rosales.

In August, when Facile and I came near the adobe one evening, I could see my mother and father sitting on the *porche*. Father was waving a piece of paper around and speaking animatedly with mother. I could just overhear bits and pieces of what he said and so I stopped at the crest of the plateau out of view and listened.

" … will not accept charity … if they are your relatives … what if … back home?"

And then mother said, "They are … successful … law …"

I wanted to hear more and so Facile and I crested the plateau and stood next to the bench where my father would occasionally come to gaze over the fields. Mother noticed me and nodded in my direction so that father would see me. He took the paper he had been waving around, folded it, and put it in his shirt pocket.

"Hello, *mijo*, where have you been?" he asked. I motioned with my hand toward the bosque.

"Come here, Chuy," said my mother. "We need to talk with you." My father's head snapped back to her with an angry sneer. "I don't care, Papa. We can't keep this secret any longer. He needs to know. Come here, *mijo*, and sit." She pulled one of the stools over next to her. My father just stared at her.

"We haven't decided!" he yelled suddenly. "I cannot pay them!" As I walked to the small table where they sat, my father got up and walked away, brushing passed me as he went to sit on the bench overlooking the fields.

"Don't mind him, *mijo*. He only … it is his pride." She looked for the paper they had been reading and then remembered that my father had put it in his pocket. She waved her hand as though dismissing its importance. I sat and Facile wandered around to his stall in the back to await his evening small hay feed.

My mother reached for my hands and held them tenderly. "Chuy, I'm sorry that we have been so secretive over the last few months, but it has been necessary. We couldn't be sure … that is to say … I …" She placed my hands, palms down, on the table with her own over them. "I'm just going to tell you straight out."

What could it be? Was someone coming to visit? Was there trouble with the farm? Were Mia Tia and her family having trouble? All the possibilities that had run through my brain resurfaced faster than I could suppress them.

"We are sending you to live with Mia Tia and her family …." That was all I heard. They are sending me away. I am a burden. But why is Papa angry? Does he want me to stay? I glanced toward my father, and mother understood why.

"It is his pride, Chuy. He wants to pay for your room and board, and we cannot …"

They won't take me unless they get paid? My own Papa will pay someone to take me away from him? This was only getting worse. My face must have shown my sadness.

"Oh, *mijo*!" My mother's voice cracked with emotion. "We are not sending you away because we don't want you!" She sobbed and pulled her handkerchief from her sleeve. "We love you … we all do, but … but … there is no life here for you."

The tears were dribbling down my cheeks and I disgustedly wiped them away, leaving a muddy smear from the dirt that was on my hands. I was sad, but a little angry, too. I started to speak, but a sob escaped my mouth with a little hiccup. "Nobody here loves me and don't you say they do! You all fit together, but I am always left out!" My mother shook her head in denial, but I

Made in the USA
Coppell, TX
05 December 2021

67132240R00017